D0186797

THIS WALKER BOOK BELONGS TO:

_____

_____

_____

For Lucy   M.D.

For Lucy and Dee, I grew   C.C.

First published 2003 by Walker Books Ltd
87 Vauxhall Walk, London SEII 5HJ

This edition published 2004

10 9 8 7 6 5 4 3 2 1

Text © 2003 Malachy Doyle
Illustrations © 2003 Carll Cneut

The right of Malachy Doyle and Carll Cneut to be identified as author and illustrator respectively of this work has been asserted by them in accordance with the Copyright, Designs and Patents Act 1988

This book has been typeset in Mrs Eaves

Printed in China

British Library Cataloguing in Publication Data:
a catalogue record for this book is available from the British Library

ISBN 1-84428-496-4

www.walkerbooks.co.uk

Antonio

on the Other Side
of the World, Getting Smaller

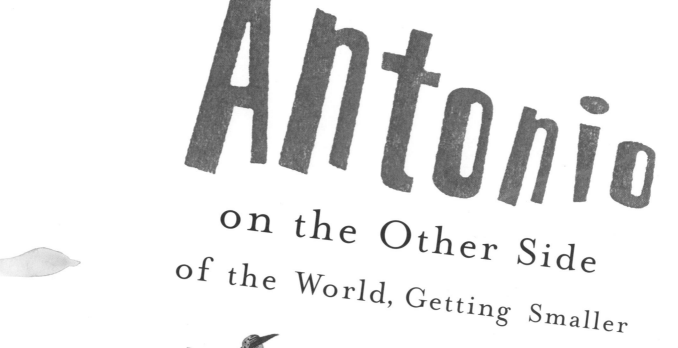

illustrated by

MALACHY DOYLE ◇ CARLL CNEUT

WALKER BOOKS
AND SUBSIDIARIES
LONDON · BOSTON · SYDNEY · AUCKLAND

Antonio went to visit his lovely gran,

on a tiny island on the other side of the world.

They had a whale of a time, paddling around in Granny's boat,

and tossing jam sandwiches to the snippy-snappy sea monsters.

But after a week and a bundle of fun,
Antonio couldn't reach the
oars any more.

And after another week,
and another bundle of fun,
he couldn't even see over
the side of the boat.

"It's lovely having you to stay, Antonio," said Gran.

"But you're only half the size you were when you came.

You're missing your mum, that's the problem.

Missing your mum and it's time you went home."

So his granny made him up another big bag of jam sandwiches,

kissed the top of his sweet little head, and away he went.

Antonio got a job on a ship,

sailing for home.

"You're a bit small for a cabin boy,"

said the crabby old captain.

"But I suppose you'll do."

It was hard work
and rough seas, but
"I'm on the way home!"
sang Antonio happily.
"For I want to be home with my mother!"

Little Antonio reached dry land at last,

but by now he was smaller still.

A whole heap smaller.

"You're a bit little for an engine boy,"
said the train driver. "But I'll see
if I can find you a job."

So Antonio rode up front
to watch out for sheep on the line.
"I'm on the way home!" he cried to the sheep.
"I'm on the way home to my mother!"

And he blasted a blast on
the whistle. *"Wheeee!"*

When Antonio got off the train he spotted a cowboy,

climbing down from a hard day in the saddle.

"Do you think I could have a ride on your horse, sir?"

said little Antonio. *"For I'm on the way home,"*

he sang, with a smile, *"I'm on the way home to my mother."*

"You're a bit small for a cowboy,"

said the man, peering down at him.

"But you can borrow my horse if you'd like.

She's far too lively for me."

So up Antonio jumped
and off he galloped.

"Yes, I'm on the way home!"

he cried as he rode.

"I'm on the way home to my mother!"

And he hung on tightly, did the brave Antonio,

till he'd ridden the range and tamed the wild horse, too.

Though by now he was only a titch of a thing,

what with being away from home so long.

Finally, finally, Antonio got to his house,

but he was so tiny that his mother

didn't notice him.

"Hello, Ma!" he squeaked, but she couldn't

even see him, and she hardly even heard him.

"What's that?" she said, looking all around.

"Is it a mouse?"

"It's me, your son!" cried Antonio, pulling on her skirts.

"Who's there?" said his mother.

"Is it an imp?"

Till little Antonio jumped up on the table,
right in front of her eyes, and yelled,
"It's me, Antonio, home at last!"

Well, wasn't she amazed at
the sight of her son — home
from afar, but oh, so small!
She hugged him and kissed him,
put him on her knee and said,
"It's great to have you back, love,
though you could do with
a bit of fattening-up."

So she fed him bread and she
fed him milk, she fed him meat
and she fed him carrots,
she fed him cake and she
fed him porridge,
till he grew,
and he grew
and he grew.

Till in time he was so tall that he

could sit on his roof, shout,

"IT'S GOOD TO BE HOME!"

and wave to his lovely gran on the

other side of the world.

And his granny waved back.

WALKER BOOKS is the world's leading independent publisher of children's books. Working with the best authors and illustrators we create books for all ages, from babies to teenagers – books your child will grow up with and always remember. So…